Puffin Island

Kim and Tim like birds.
They have always liked birds.
Puffin Island is a bird island —
no houses, no people,
just lots and lots of birds.

The warden lets the boys visit the
island to help him count the birds.

When the tide is out they can walk across to the island, but when the tide comes in it is too deep to get across.

The boys like to sit in the warden's hide, counting and drawing the birds. They can see the birds making their nests and sitting on their eggs.

Puffin Island is for birds, not people, so no tents or fires or litter are allowed.

The boys had been counting and
drawing for a long time, when...

As the boat came near
the boys could see three men.

They landed on the sand,
and started walking up the beach!

The two boys ducked down,
and stayed very still.
They could hear the men talking.

"Did you hear that?" whispered Kim.
"Yes, they are going to steal some
 eggs from the nests," whispered Tim,
"but we must stop them!
We can't let them get away with it!"

"But how can we stop three big men?"
whispered Kim.
"We need help, and the warden
won't be back for a long time."
The boys felt glum. How could they
stop the men and save the eggs?

10

Kim had an idea.
"You run along the beach,
and I'll get help," he said.
"But how? Now the tide is in
we can't get across the water!"
said Tim.

"We don't have time to talk," said
Kim. "You just get the men away
from the nest and I'll do the rest."

Tim ran along the beach,
as fast as he could.

Kim got out of the back of the hide.
He found lots of dry twigs and
leaves, and ran down to the boat.

13

"Look Dad, over there — it's smoke!"
said Ali. "Kim and Tim went to
Puffin Island today, and they never
light fires on the island.
They must need help!"

"Quick! Go and call up the warden
on our radio," said his dad.

"Quick!" shouted the warden,
"It's the gang we've been trying to
catch for weeks!"

"Well done boys," said the warden.
"You saved the Snowy Owl's eggs.
That is one fire I'm *very* pleased
you lit on Puffin Island!
From now on, you can be my
assistant wardens for Puffin Island!"